Zanzibar

Zanzibar

Catharina Valckx

Illustrations by the author
Translated by Antony Shugaar

GECKO PRESS

Chapter 1

Zanzibar had just begun dinner when there was a knock at the door.

It was a lizard in glasses.

"*Bonjour*," said the lizard. "I'm Achille LeBlab, special correspondent. I wonder if I could ask you a few questions?"

He doesn't look dangerous, Zanzibar thought. He let the reporter in.

The lizard settled into the best armchair.

"First of all," he said, "your name."

"Zanzibar," said Zanzibar.

"Zanzibar? Like the African island?"

"That's right. Like the island."

"Very nice," said the lizard.

He licked a finger and leafed through his notepad.

"I'm writing a feature for my newspaper. I'm looking for exceptional characters. Do you do anything out of the ordinary?"

Zanzibar stopped to think.

"Like, for instance, can you sing?"
asked the lizard.

"Well...yes."

"There you go! If you can sing as
sweetly as the nightingale, I'll write an
article about you."

"CAW! CAW! CAW! CAW!" Zanzibar
sang.

"Do you call that singing, that
mournful croaking?"

Zanzibar shrugged. This reporter was starting to get on his nerves. What's more, his dinner was getting cold.

"Zanzibar-r-r…" said the lizard, rolling the r with an air of inspiration. "Would you happen to be a champion at anything at all?"

Zanzibar shot a glance at his plate.

"I'm very good at mushroom omelettes."

The lizard burst out laughing.

"Omelettes! How quaint! But I'm afraid, my good man, I don't think that would interest our readers."

Zanzibar said nothing.

"Oh well, apart from your very poetic name, I'm sorry to say you're a rather ordinary crow," the lizard concluded as he capped his pen. "I'll leave you to your omelette."

"Fine," said Zanzibar a little coldly.

"But here's my card. You never know."

Zanzibar slammed the door. His omelette was ruined. Not that it mattered. The visit had spoiled his appetite anyway.

He stepped over to the lamp and examined the lizard's card.

ACHILLE LeBLAB
Special Correspondent
The Voice of the Forest

The Voice of the Forest, Zanzibar thought to himself, must be a very important newspaper.

That reporter will probably write an article about the nightingale. And about the fox, who's a chess champion. And maybe about Ginette, the frog, who once dived into the pond from the top of a tree...

Zanzibar got into bed. He fluffed up his pillow sadly.

"I would have liked to be in the newspaper. But I'm just ordinary. As ordinary as a crow can be."

He switched off the light and tried to sleep. He couldn't stop thinking about Achille LeBlab.

"He left his card. He could see that I'm a crow with enormous potential."

Zanzibar suddenly sat bolt upright and spoke aloud: "I haven't done anything remarkable yet, but it's never too late! I'm going... I'm going to lift a camel! That's it! I'll lift a camel in the air with just one wing!"

Chapter 2

The next morning, Paulette the mole called on her friend Zanzibar. He told her about his visit from Achille LeBlab.

"And so, I'm going to lift a camel with a single wing," he concluded.

"Do you think I'll be a remarkable crow if I manage to do that?"

"Of course!" Paulette exclaimed. "But where will you find a camel?"

"Hmmm...I think they live by the sea."

"No, that's not right," said Paulette. "I went to the seaside once. I didn't see a single camel."

Knock knock knock!

Zanzibar opened the door.

"*Bonjour*, Monsieur Seagull. Is there a letter for me?"

"No," said the mailman, "I knocked just to tell you there's nothing for you today."

"Thanks," said Zanzibar. "Do you happen to know where camels live?"

Monsieur Seagull scratched his head under his cap.

"I think they live in the desert."

"And where exactly is the desert?"

"That way." Monsieur Seagull pointed south. "Far, far away."

"How far?"

"Several days' flying."

"Several days!" Zanzibar exclaimed. "I'd better get going at once then."

Chapter 3

Zanzibar packed a backpack and
headed south.

A camel, he thought along the way,
is almost the same as a dromedary.
Except that a camel has two humps and
a dromedary only one. Which means

that a dromedary must surely be a little
lighter. That said, it would be easier to
lift a very small camel than an enormous
dromedary. The ideal would be a very
small, skinny dromedary.

Chapter 4

At last, Zanzibar reached the desert. Nothing but sand dunes as far as the eye could see.

The dromedaries might be hiding under the dunes, he thought.

He was nibbling on a cupcake when a fennec fox happened along.

"Hello," said the fennec. "You're not from here, are you?"

"No," said Zanzibar, "I'm looking for a very small, skinny dromedary."

"To do what with?"

"To lift it with a single wing."

The fennec fox raised an eyebrow.

"I know of one, an extremely slender dromedary. Come with me!"

He led Zanzibar to a tent.

A very small, skinny dromedary
wearing socks welcomed them in.

"Hello, Cheb," said the fennec fox,
"I've brought you a visitor."

"Come in, come in," said the dromedary. "But make sure you shake all the sand off your feet. To what do I owe the pleasure of this visit?"

"I'd like to lift you up in the air," Zanzibar replied, a little nervous now. "If you wouldn't mind."

"With just one wing," the fennec fox added.

"Lift me up in the air? Why not," said Cheb. "But not right now. It's my nap time."

And with that, he stretched out on the carpet and shut his eyes.

"Come to my house while we wait
for him to wake up," said the fennec fox.
"I have some desert-rose tea."

The fennec fox lived in a big cactus.

He showed Zanzibar in, and served the tea in very small glasses.

"I'm Sidi. And you?"

"Zanzibar," said Zanzibar.

"What do you think of my tea?"

"It tastes of pebbles," Zanzibar said frankly.

"Really?" Sidi was astonished. "You can't taste the rose petals?"

Zanzibar took another gulp.

"No, more like gravel."

"It's because you're not used to it," said Sidi. "Add a little sugar."

To pass the time, they told each other stories. Stories of the desert and stories of the forest.

Chapter 5

Sidi and Zanzibar returned to the tent.

Cheb was busy shaking out his carpet.

He laid it carefully back inside the tent, then stood in the middle of it.

"There you are," he said, "I'm all yours."

Zanzibar put down his backpack. He positioned himself between the dromedary's hoofs and lifted a wing toward the skinny belly.

"Hee-hee! You're tickling me with your feathers," Cheb chuckled.

Zanzibar took a deep breath and pushed with all his might.

"He's not budging," said Sidi.

Zanzibar clamped his beak shut. His wing grew numb.

Discouraged, he let himself drop to the carpet.

"Are you sure he didn't lift me even a hair's breadth?" Cheb asked.

"Nothing, not the tiniest bit," Sidi sighed.

Poor Zanzibar dissolved in tears.

"I'll never be able to do it. I'm too short."

"*Too short?*" Sidi leapt to his feet. "Is that all?"

He ran from the tent and soon returned with a footstool under his arm.

"Stand on this," he told Zanzibar.

Zanzibar climbed up.

"There," Sidi declared triumphantly. "You're not too short. You can do it now. I even brought my camera."

"It's now or never," Zanzibar told himself.

He concentrated. He lifted one wing, flexed his knees, bent his back, and pushed. He pushed as if his life depended on it.

"Come on!" Sidi encouraged him.

The stool tilted, but it didn't fall. And suddenly the miracle occurred. Cheb's socks rose from the carpet.

"You've lifted him!" Sidi shouted. He snapped the camera shutter.

Click click click.

Zanzibar thought he must be dreaming.

"I did it," he murmured proudly. "Is that even possible?"

"Good work." Sidi threw his arms around him. "Bravo and well done."

"Congratulations," said Cheb. "I really enjoyed that little session. It's not every day I get to take off from my carpet. I'd like to give you a gift, for a souvenir."

He sat down and took off one of his socks.

"Here, this is for you. My grandmother knitted it."

Zanzibar thanked him.

"A cup of tea, to celebrate?" Sidi
offered.

"No, thanks," said Zanzibar.

"Come back whenever you like," said
Cheb.

Zanzibar bade farewell to his new
friends and flew away home.

Chapter 6

Back in the forest, Zanzibar went straight over to Paulette's house.

"I did it!" he proudly announced.

Paulette gazed with admiration. "Really? You lifted a camel with just one wing?"

"A dromedary. He gave me a souvenir. Look."

Zanzibar opened his backpack and pulled out the sock. Paulette took it from him.

"It's oddly beautiful. But it smells of camel."

"Of dromedary," Zanzibar corrected her.

"It's still full of sand!"

Zanzibar thought back to all that sand, down there in the desert. He thought of Cheb's tent, and of Sidi...

Paulette looked at him.

"You've changed," she said. "You have the look of a great adventurer."

Zanzibar was so happy, he broke into song.

After lunch, Zanzibar went over to *The Voice of the Forest.*

Achille LeBlab received him in a small smoke-filled office.

"How are you, Zanzibar, my friend? There's a sparkle in your eye."

"The truth is I've done something remarkable," said Zanzibar.

"Ah!" said the lizard. He tried to open his desk drawer, but it was stuck.

He gave it a kick and pulled out his notepad.

"Tell me about it."

"I lifted a dromedary in the air with a single wing," Zanzibar declared.

Achille LeBlab pushed his glasses
back on his nose.

"You lifted a what?"

"A dromedary."

"Listen," said the lizard, as he put
down his pen, "a little imagination,
a little flair, that's fine. But a crow lifting
a dromedary, no. Don't take my readers
for utter fools."

"But it's true!" Zanzibar protested.

"It's impossible, you're too small," Achille LeBlab said, categorically.

"I know that," said Zanzibar, "but I stood on a stool."

Achille LeBlab frowned.

"So that's it. Plus you drank a magic potion."

"Well...no. Actually, it was tea."

"Right. Well, if you'll be so good as to excuse me, Monsieur Zanzi-barefaced-liar, I have work to do."

The lizard pushed Zanzibar toward the door.

"And don't bother me again with your fairy tales!"

Furious, Zanzibar set out for home.
The sky was clouded over. It was about
to rain.

Ginette the frog came along.

"Zanzibar!" she exclaimed happily, "I have something to tell you."

Zanzibar walked over reluctantly.

"Listen," said Ginette, bouncing on the spot in excitement. "A special correspondent is going to write a whole story about me! Because I leaped into the pond from the top of the weeping willow. Do you remember?"

"Yes, I remember," said Zanzibar gloomily. "Lucky you. He doesn't believe my story, though."

Ginette stopped bouncing.

"Why, did you do something exceptional, too?"

"I lifted a dromedary with a single wing."

Ginette gaped.

"A real one?"

"Oh, not a big one," said Zanzibar.

Ginette slapped him on the back.

"You're pulling my leg."

Suddenly the rain started pouring down, like a firehose aiming straight out of the sky.

Zanzibar ran for shelter.

Chapter 7

Back at home, Zanzibar dried his feathers and cooked a mushroom omelette. But his heart wasn't in it. The omelette was half charred. Inedible.

He stretched out on his bed, but only dark thoughts came to him.

"I'll write a letter to Sidi," he decided.
He took out paper and pen.

Dear Sidi

The pen was almost out of ink.
Zanzibar had to press hard and go over
each word three times.

It's raining here. I just ruined
an omelette. That's never happened
to me before.

The pen was now entirely out of ink.
He was rummaging in his closet for
another one when Paulette tapped at the
window.

"What filthy weather!" She sniffed
the air. "Something's burning."

"The reporter showed me the door,"
Zanzibar said sadly. "He doesn't believe
me. I did it all for nothing."

Paulette leaned over the stove. She
picked at the bottom of the pan.

"You know, Zanzibar, none of that
really matters."

"You mean the newspaper?"

"Yes. I know perfectly well how
remarkable you are. You already were,
before you lifted the camel."

"The *dromedary*," Zanzibar sighed.

"Right. But I'm worried about
something far more serious."

"What's that?"

Zanzibar was suddenly uneasy, too.

"About your skills as a chef." Paulette held up the pan, laughing. "Now that you're going off to distant lands to lift large mammals in the air, you're forgetting how to cook!"

Zanzibar couldn't help smiling a little.

"Look, here's the mailman. *Bonjour,* Monsieur Seagull. Nothing, as usual?"

"Something!" Monsieur Seagull rushed into the house. "A package with unusual stamps. If you don't mind, I'll stay while you open it."

Zanzibar examined the package.

"These are stamps from the desert!"

He ripped off the brown wrapping paper and found a cardboard box.

"Open it!"

Paulette was beside herself with curiosity.

Zanzibar cautiously lifted the lid.

"Sand," he said, disappointed.

"Look under the sand," said Monsieur Seagull, expert that he is.

Zanzibar scrabbled through the sand with his feathers.

"I can feel something..."

There was a photograph buried in the sand.

And a small letter.

"It's a photo of my triumph!"

Heart racing, Zanzibar read the letter:

Dear Zanzibar,

The photos came out very nicely. I gave one to Cheb and he hung it in his tent. He talks about you every time I see him. I hope (and so does he) that you'll come back to see us soon. Since you don't much like my tea, I've laid in a stock of cactus syrup. I'll keep it for you.

Hugs to you,
Sidi.

Glowing with happiness, Zanzibar read and reread Sidi's letter.

"That photo really did come out well," said Paulette. "Let's take it straight over to *The Voice of the Forest*. That Monsieur LeBlab is in for a surprise!"

But Zanzibar wasn't listening. He was looking for a pen that worked.

"Come on," Paulette insisted. "What are you doing?"

"I'm going to write back to Sidi," said Zanzibar. "I'm so glad he wrote to me! It was really kind. Sidi and Cheb are both so nice. Someday I'll take you to visit them."

Paulette furrowed her brow.

"But Zanzibar, the newspaper comes out tomorrow! You've done something remarkable, and that photograph proves it. If you don't take it straight over there, it'll be too late."

"Too bad," said Zanzibar. "It's not important, you said so yourself. I want to write to my friends."

Monsieur Seagull smiled.

"Ah, letters!"

Paulette reached for her umbrella, grabbed the photo, and ran from the house.

Chapter 8

The next morning, Zanzibar slept in.

Monsieur Seagull knocked on the window. He hammered the glass with his knuckles.

"Okay, okay, take it easy!" Zanzibar yelled as he tumbled out of bed.

He opened the door and looked in astonishment at the old mailman, who was gesticulating wildly.

"You...this is brilliant...your..."

Monsieur Seagull was overexcited. He could hardly speak.

"You'd better come in," Zanzibar said.

Monsieur Seagull tried to pull something from his mailbag, which was packed with letters. Half the mail was on the ground by the time he finally brandished the newspaper.

Zanzibar blinked. His picture was on the front page of *The Voice of the Forest.* It was huge. Above it was a big headline that read:

INCREDIBLE ZANZIBAR

And beneath the photograph, there was an article:

Of all the inhabitants of our forest, the one who most deserves our admiration is the crow with the lovely name of Zanzibar.

Zanzibar went into the desert with the sole objective of doing something noteworthy. There, he lifted a dromedary into the air on a single wing! Zanzibar performed this absurd feat simply for the beauty of the gesture and to entertain us all.

Thank you, Zanzibar!

The article was signed: Achille LeBlab.

"It was Paulette who took in the photo," Monsieur Seagull explained. "Zanzibar, you're famous!"

"You think so?"

Suddenly Paulette threw open the door and wrapped her arms around her friend's neck.

"Did you see? Are you happy?"

And the next thing Zanzibar knew, Ginette was bouncing into the kitchen to congratulate him. Then the fox, the nightingale, the hare, the ant, the tortoise, the mosquito, the owl— everyone wanted to hug their hero. Even Madame Adele, the moth, came hobbling in on her crutches. The kitchen was full to bursting.

Zanzibar was confused. Being famous was all very well, but when it catches you unprepared—just like that, when you're scarcely out of bed—it can be a little awkward.

He sidled over to Paulette and whispered: "What should I do now?"

"I don't know," she said, "you could make a speech."

"A speech!" Zanzibar moaned. "No, I'd much rather make a mushroom omelette."

Chapter 9

Zanzibar's omelette was delicious. Madame Adele couldn't get enough and asked for thirds.

"So, tell me, Zanzibar," she said between mouthfuls, "this dromedary you lifted, was it very skinny?"

"Very, very skinny," said Zanzibar.

"Now be perfectly frank. Do you think I could lift him, too?"

Zanzibar almost choked on the mouthful he was swallowing.

"Why not, Madame Adele," he said with a laugh. "But you'd better hurry, because I sent him my omelette recipe."

"Ah, then I'm too late," the old lady sighed. "He can't help but put on weight now."

"Absolutely," Paulette agreed.

She lifted her glass.

"Here's to you, our dear, incredible Zanzibar!"

"To your health!" exclaimed Madame Adele.

"To Zanzibar!" the whole table shouted.

Deeply moved, Zanzibar glanced at the sock hanging on the wall.

"To all my friends!"

This edition first published in 2019 by Gecko Press
PO Box 9335, Wellington 6141, New Zealand
info@geckopress.com

English-language edition © Gecko Press Ltd 2019
Translation © Antony Shugaar 2019
Reprinted 2020

Original title: *L'incroyable Zanzibar*
Text and illustrations by Catharina Valckx
© 2003 l'école des loisirs, Paris

Edited by Penelope Todd
Design and typesetting by Katrina Duncan
Printed in China by Everbest Printing Co. Ltd,
an accredited ISO 14001 & FSC-certified printer

MIX
Paper from
responsible sources
FSC FSC® C124385
www.fsc.org

ISBN hardback: 978-1-776572-55-7 (USA)
ISBN paperback: 978-1-776572-56-4
Ebook available

For more curiously good books, visit geckopress.com